JAKE MADDOX

ADVENTURE

TRAIL TROUBLE

BY JAKE MADDOX

3 1336 11079 5904

Text by Shawn Pryor

Illustrated by Alan Brown

STONE ARCH BOOKS
a capstone imprint

Jake Maddox Adventure is published by Stone Arch Books,
an imprint of Capstone.
1710 Roe Crest Drive
North Mankato, Minnesota 56003
www.capstonepub.com

Library of Congress Cataloging-in-Publication Data is available on
the Library of Congress website.

ISBN: 978-1-4965-8694-0 (hardcover)
ISBN: 978-1-4965-9203-3 (paperback)
ISBN: 978-1-4965-8695-7 (eBook PDF)

Summary: On a summer vacation with his family, Marlon Keys is
about to hike the Appalachian Trail. He isn't exactly thrilled about
the trip—he'd rather play on his smartphone and connect with his
friends back home. But when Marlon and another hiker named Nadia
accidentally get separated from the group on the hike, his "boring"
vacation becomes an exercise in survival.

Cover illustration by Giuliano Aloisi

Designer: Lori Bye

Printed in the United States of America.
PA100

TABLE OF CONTENTS

CHAPTER 1

HIKING

"Marlon Anthony Keys, turn off your phone and listen to what your father and I are trying to tell you," Mom said from the front seat of the family SUV. "We'll be at Shenandoah National Park soon."

"OK, OK, fine," twelve-year-old Marlon grumbled. He rolled his eyes at his friend on the other end of the video chat. "Troy, I have to hang up. My parents are forcing me to go hiking and camping with them on some dumb trail."

"The Appalachian Trail, dear," Mom retorted.

Troy looked surprised. "The Appalachian Trail? That sounds so cool!"

Marlon snorted. "What's so cool about it? I'm going to miss your birthday party because we have to go wander around in the woods and do some bird-watching."

"This trip is more than just looking at birds," Dad corrected as he navigated down the highway. "It's about us spending time together, learning, and enjoying the wonders of nature."

"I can enjoy the wonders of nature in our backyard," Marlon joked. "Couldn't we have just roasted marshmallows there?"

"That's it, hang up right now, or I'm taking your phone away for the rest of the trip!" Mom said. "You've already missed so much of the wonderful scenery because you've been on your phone the whole drive."

Marlon sighed. They'd been in the car for hours—ever since leaving Chicago at the crack of dawn. The last thing he wanted to do was go on a trip through the wilderness. It would be even worse if he had to do it without his phone.

"Later, Troy," Marlon muttered.

"Later!" Troy said as he ended the call.

Marlon put his phone away and sighed again. "I don't see what the big deal is about walking in the woods. It's just a bunch of trees and bugs out there. We could be doing something way cooler instead. Why this?"

"The great outdoors is more than just trees and bugs," Mom said. "And hiking can be more dangerous than you think. You need to pay attention or you could put yourself at serious risk."

"I doubt it," Marlon muttered under his breath.

"What was that?" Dad said.

"Nothing," Marlon said, turning to stare out the window. As far as he was concerned, the sooner this trip was over, the better.

CHAPTER 2

WHAT'S THE BIG DEAL?

Three hours later, the Keys family finally arrived at Shenandoah National Park. Dad parked the car, and everyone climbed out.

Marlon stood and stretched his legs. He was glad to finally be out of the car, even if they did seem to be in the middle of nowhere.

Mom and Dad grabbed the hiking gear. Marlon struggled to put on his backpack. It was harder than he'd expected.

"Why do they make these things so hard to put on?" he whined.

"We tried to show you how to put your pack on before we left home, but you couldn't be bothered," Dad said.

"I was busy," Marlon grumbled.

"Yeah, too busy to even pack your own bag," Mom retorted. "I had to do it for you. It's like you don't even appreciate this vacation."

"You need to adjust your attitude," Dad said. "You're too attached to your phone. Maybe if you unplugged sometimes you'd see the health benefits."

Marlon didn't say anything. He was sick of his parents always giving him a hard time about being on his phone. How else was he supposed to talk to his friends?

After a few more minutes of struggling with the straps, Marlon finally managed to get his backpack on. It weighed a ton. Together, he and his parents headed to the rangers' office. As they entered, a uniformed man greeted them.

"Good afternoon!" he said, smiling at them. "I'm Ranger James. Welcome to Shenandoah National Park, one part of the massive Appalachian Trail. Checking in?"

"Yes," said Marlon's dad. "We're the Keys family."

"Ah, I've been expecting you. You're all set up for a cabin share with the Sharma family," Ranger James said. "Follow me, and I'll introduce you to them."

Marlon rolled his eyes. *We have to share a room with another family? Ugh. Great, more people I don't want to be around.*

Ranger James led Marlon and his parents out of the office and down a winding, rutted dirt trail. Lush chestnut trees lined the path.

As they walked, Marlon saw a spider sitting in the middle of a massive web. The creature sat suspended between two of the chestnut trees.

Ugh, I hate bugs, Marlon thought with a shiver. Just seeing the spider made him itch uncomfortably.

A few moments later, they arrived at the cabin. Marlon looked at the run-down living quarters and sighed. The covered front porch housed a set of dusty old rocking chairs, and an outdoor fireplace was set up a few feet away. The cabin was definitely big enough for two families, but not big enough for Marlon to have space for himself.

Hopefully this place has electricity, he thought.

"Here we are," Ranger James said. "Cabin fifteen." He opened the door to the cabin. Inside, another family was already settling in.

"Keys family, meet the Sharmas," Ranger James said. "I'm sure you're all tired from traveling, but there's a chance we might have some storms tomorrow on your group hike. Let's discuss some tips for hiking in bad weather after you've finished settling in."

As Marlon's parents greeted the other adults, a girl who looked to be about Marlon's age walked over.

"Hi," she said. "I'm Nadia."

"Nice to meet you," Marlon replied. "I'm Marlon. Did your parents drag you on this trip too?"

Nadia shook her head. "It was actually my idea," she said. "This is my fourth hiking trip, but I've never been on the trail before. What about you? Are you a big hiker too?"

Great, Marlon thought. *Another outdoor enthusiast.*

He shook his head. "Nope. But it looks like I don't have much of a choice, do I?"

Before Nadia could respond, Ranger James addressed the group again.

"You're all scheduled to take a group hike on the trail tomorrow," he said, "so make sure to use your maps to stay on the safe pathways."

I'd rather stay off all *pathways,* Marlon thought. He resisted the urge to roll his eyes.

"It's up to your group if you plan to do an up-and-back or camp overnight on the trail," the ranger continued. He studied both families. "Does everyone here know what 'up-and-back' means?"

Nadia raised her hand. "It's when you turn around and retrace your steps, heading back to where you started, on a hike," she replied.

"That's right!" said Ranger James. "You should also be prepared tomorrow if thunderstorms roll through while you're on the trail. Make sure you have the essentials: water, poncho, snacks, flashlight, first-aid kit, and your tent."

"Can't we just come back if it rains?" Marlon asked. "Or use our phones to call for help?"

Ranger James nodded. "Some folks enjoy the experience of camping in the rain, but if the storms are really bad, I would suggest coming back to your cabin," he said. "But as for the second part of your question, there's no cell phone reception out on the trail. Using your phone out there is a waste of time."

Marlon's mother turned toward him and winked. "Did you hear that, Marlon? You'll have to live without your phone tomorrow."

Marlon shrugged. "We're only walking through the woods," he said. "I think I'll survive."

CHAPTER 3

WRONG TURN

The next day, the two families woke up early. Everyone except Marlon seemed eager for the group hike on the Appalachian Trail. Everyone loaded up their packs and set off through the oak-hickory forest. The adults walked together in the front, while Marlon and Nadia brought up the rear.

The group hiked past clusters of colorful mushrooms and patches of moss that grew on the trees. Massive rocks lay on the trail. Ferns and freshwater plants lined the route. The leaves from the red oaks in the forest glistened in the sun.

Everyone seemed impressed by the beauty of the trail. Marlon, however, was not pleased. Thirty minutes into the three-hour hike, he just wanted to go home.

"Does anyone want to guess how many states the Appalachian Trail runs through?" Mr. Sharma called back from the front of the group.

The parents turned and looked at Marlon and Nadia. Marlon shrugged his shoulders.

"Technically, the Appalachian Trail cuts through as many as fourteen states from start to finish," Nadia piped up.

"Figures you would know," Marlon muttered.

"When I was younger, my dad would take me and the entire family hiking," Marlon's dad said loudly. "We loved it so much. It was a tradition that I wanted to continue with our family. I can't believe I waited so long to do it."

"That's very sweet," said Mrs. Sharma.

The families continued along the trail. As the adults chatted, they slowly pulled ahead of the kids.

Nadia studied the ground. "Watch your step, Marlon," she said. "There are a lot of roots on this part of the path."

Marlon didn't reply. At first Nadia thought he was just being rude. But when she looked up, she found him sitting on a log at the side of the trail, picking fungus off it.

"C'mon, Marlon, we should catch up with our parents," Nadia said, walking over. The adults had disappeared around a bend in the trail. "Marlon?"

"Ugh, I don't want to be here at all. I hate hiking," Marlon grumbled.

"How can you hate something you've never tried? Give it a chance. Hiking can be a lot of fun," said Nadia.

"Easy for you to say. You like this stuff. I got dragged here—and I'm missing out on hanging with my friends because of it. Just leave me alone," Marlon snarled.

Nadia glared at him. "Fine. Stay here then." She turned and walked away.

"I will!" Marlon replied. He huffed, glad to be left alone. But a moment later, there was a rustling noise in the brush.

What was that? Marlon thought. *Who's there?*

Suddenly a squirrel leapt from the brush and bounced off of Marlon's head. Marlon panicked. He jumped up from the log and raced after Nadia. The squirrel chased after Marlon.

"Wait for me!" Marlon called. He ran toward—and quickly past—Nadia. There was a fork in the trail up ahead, and he veered left.

"Hey, slow down!" Nadia hollered. She watched in shock as the squirrel continued its pursuit of Marlon. "You're going down the wrong trail! Our parents went this way!"

Marlon didn't listen. With a sigh, Nadia took off after him. She was so focused on catching up to him that she wasn't watching where she was going.

Before she knew it, Nadia tripped on a root. She slid off the narrow trail and tumbled down a large, sloped hill. She tumbled down the steep incline covered in ferns and grass. As she fell, Nadia caught sight of Marlon, lying very still at the bottom of the hill.

CHAPTER 4

WHAT ARE WE GOING TO DO?

At the bottom of the hill, Nadia climbed to her feet. "Are you OK?" she asked Marlon. She walked over and checked him for injuries.

Marlon winced as she poked and prodded, but luckily, nothing seemed broken. He'd survived with just a few minor scratches.

"No, I'm not OK," Marlon snapped. "A wild animal tried to eat me—"

"Oh, you mean the squirrel that was chasing you down the trail?" Nadia said, rolling her eyes. She brushed the dirt off her clothes and removed her backpack to make sure everything was still intact.

Marlon glared at her as he stood up. "It's not my fault. I tripped over a stupid root," he argued.

"It kind of is your fault," Nadia said. "If you'd stayed with the group, we wouldn't be in this situation. Now our parents have no idea where we are."

"So we'll call for help," Marlon said. He pulled his smartphone from his pocket. "Come on, connect! Why can't I get a signal out here?" He held his phone in the air.

"The ranger told us yesterday that our phones wouldn't work out here," said Nadia. "Were you even listening?"

Marlon didn't reply. "Mom! Dad! Can anyone hear me?" he yelled.

"We're too far off the trail. Our parents can't hear us," Nadia said.

"So let's climb back up the hill then," Marlon said.

Nadia pointed at the hill. "There's no way we can climb back up. It's too steep," she said.

She was right, Marlon realized. The hill they'd fallen down *was* steep and covered in slick grass. There was nowhere along the fern-covered incline to get a grip or foothold. It seemed to stretch on like that for miles.

Suddenly thunder rattled and the clouds began to roll in. Nadia and Marlon looked up. Raindrops started to slowly fall.

Nadia pulled out her poncho and put it on. Marlon struggled to take off his backpack so he could check the contents. He realized he had no idea what was in there.

"Where is it? Where's my rain thingy?" Marlon said.

"You mean your poncho?" Nadia said.

"I have to have one! This is the worst day of my life! I have no idea what I'm doing out here." Marlon continued to panic.

Nadia tried to calm him. "Freaking out isn't going to help you find your poncho. Step back, take a deep breath, and I'll look for it."

"OK. OK," Marlon said. He handed Nadia his backpack and forced himself to take a deep breath.

What are we going to do? How are we going to find our parents? How are we going to get back to our cabin? he thought. *I just want to go home!*

Nadia found Marlon's poncho and tossed it to him. He quickly put it on.

"Thanks," he said. "What do we do now?"

Nadia looked up at the sky, which was now dark with storm clouds. The rain was starting to come down more steadily.

"We're going to have to pitch a tent," she said. "This storm is going to be around for a while."

CHAPTER 5

AN UNEXPECTED GUEST

Nadia and Marlon both dug through their packs. They each had a tent, but Marlon's was larger.

"Let's just pitch yours," Nadia said. "It's big enough for both of us. There's no need to put mine up too."

Marlon didn't know enough to argue, so he just nodded in agreement. Nadia prepared the poles as Marlon unrolled the tent. He struggled to insert the metal tubes into the tent and lock them in place, but with Nadia's help, he started to get the hang of it.

Wow, she really knows her stuff, Marlon thought as he watched Nadia work quickly and efficiently. *I'm lucky she's here. I'd have no clue what to do on my own.*

After thirty minutes, the tent was ready. Just in time too—the rain had turned into a torrential downpour. The kids crouched down and hurried inside the temporary shelter.

Nadia took her heat lamp from her backpack. She turned it on and placed it in the center of the tent.

"This will give us light and keep us warm," she said.

"There are some small hooks in the corner. Let's put our ponchos there," Marlon suggested.

"Good idea. We'll put our backpacks over there so they can dry off too," said Nadia. "Your parents got you a great tent."

"Yeah, I guess they did," Marlon said, glancing around. It was a blue tent, big enough for at least three people. The curved roof was almost tall enough for Marlon and Nadia to stand up in the middle. "Guess that's why my backpack was so heavy."

Nadia unrolled their sleeping bags. Marlon dug through his backpack and pulled out some trail mix filled with almonds, cashews, cranberries, and pumpkin seeds.

After taking a handful, he handed the bag to Nadia. It was the least he could do after Nadia had helped them get out of the rain.

The kids snacked silently for awhile. Finally Marlon spoke up.

"I'm sorry for the way I acted on the trail," he said. "I didn't mean to get us into this mess. Or act like such a jerk. I just didn't want to go on this trip. It's my fault we're lost."

"We'll find a way back," Nadia said as she munched on some trail mix. With her other hand, she pulled a baggie out from her back pocket. "Here, when you're done with your snacks, put them in this. It's called a bear bag. It seals the smell of food, so wild animals won't stop by."

"Oh. Thanks." Marlon placed the bag by his trail mix.

"This storm is probably going to last through the night. We should rest here until morning," said Nadia. "Then we'll look at our maps and try to figure out a way to get back."

Suddenly there was a noise outside the tent—a low scratching followed by a growl. Whatever it was sounded different from the rain or thunder.

"We should zip up the tent opening," said Nadia, glancing in that direction. Even she looked a little nervous.

"Yeah, you should do that," Marlon agreed.

"Me?" Nadia said. "It's your tent!"

"I don't want whatever's out there to get me!" Marlon said.

"Me neither!" Nadia yelled. Taking a deep breath, she exhaled. "OK. Let's just close it together."

Marlon and Nadia looked at each other. Together they slowly approached the tent opening. As they were about to reach for the zipper, lightning flashed. Whatever was outside burst into the tent and jumped on Nadia!

"Get it off of me!" Nadia yelled.

Marlon started laughing when he realized what they'd been so afraid of: a Jack Russell terrier, licking Nadia's face.

"It's just a dog," Marlon said. He grabbed the dog's harness and pulled it off Nadia. "He's probably hungry and lost, just like us."

Marlon pulled the soaking-wet dog over by the heat lamp to help him get dry. Nadia got a wipe from her backpack and wiped the dog slobber off her face.

"He's got tags," she said. "What's his name?"

Marlon checked the dog's collar. "Colt. Welcome to the squad, Colt," he said. He rubbed the dog's head. Colt wagged his tail.

Outside, loud cracks of thunder and lightning continued to crash all around. After one particularly loud *boom,* an animal howled. It didn't sound far away.

"What do you think that howling noise was?" Nadia asked.

Marlon looked worried. The tent suddenly seemed less safe and secure.

"I don't know," he said. "And I don't want to find out."

CHAPTER 6

SLEEPLESS NIGHT

In the middle of the night, the rain and thunder roared. The wind from the storm rattled the tent.

The heat lamp kept them warm, but Marlon couldn't sleep, even with Colt and Nadia in the tent. Instead, he closed his eyes and thought of all the things he should have done differently.

My parents are probably worried sick about me. I should have paid attention to them, he thought. *I should have listened to the ranger when we arrived. I should have taken this seriously.*

Marlon huddled deeper into his sleeping bag, wishing he was safe and sound with his family. Even the cabin sounded good at this point.

As he lay there, Marlon's stomach growled loudly. Trail mix hadn't been a very filling dinner.

I wish I was eating Mom's fried yuca strips and tamales right now, he thought. *I wish I was in my own bed.*

"I want to go home," Marlon whispered quietly.

"Same," Nadia said. "This tent is nice, but it's not a real bed."

Marlon hadn't realized she was awake too. Somehow that made him feel better.

"Every time I think I hear something outside, it wakes me up," he admitted. "I wonder if our parents are out in this awful weather looking for us."

"We should both try to get some sleep," Nadia said. "Tomorrow, when it's light out, we'll pull out our compasses and maps. We have to figure out where we are and how to get back."

Marlon wished he shared Nadia's confidence.

Just then, lightning struck again, followed by another loud boom of thunder. Marlon crept even deeper into his sleeping bag. His fears, meanwhile, began to creep to the surface.

But what if we don't find our way back? he worried. *What do we do then?*

CHAPTER 7

A ROOKIE MISTAKE

The next day, Marlon and Nadia woke up early. The rain had stopped, and it was time to pack up the tent and their supplies.

Nadia disconnected all the poles into smaller pieces and wrapped them together with Velcro tape. Marlon carefully folded the tent, then secured it using the tent belt straps.

Using a loose cord that was in his backpack, Marlon made a makeshift leash for Colt. He attached it to the dog's harness.

"There you go," Marlon said. "Now you won't get lost again. We'll get you back to your family."

The dog let out a whine. He seemed as anxious as Marlon felt.

"Don't forget to put your trail mix in your bear bag," Nadia reminded him. She took a drink from her canteen. "And check to see how much water you have left. I'm all out."

"OK," said Marlon. He fed Colt a handful of snacks, then set them down for a second so he could check his canteen and put on his backpack. "I'm out of water too."

"Well at least we're near a river," Nadia said. "We can fill up with fresh water."

The kids and Colt walked to the edge of the river. Colt began to lap up some water.

"I think I'll go a little upstream," Marlon said. "I don't want any dog germs in my canteen."

Nadia and Marlon took a few steps away from Colt. Nadia was about to dip her canteen into the water when Marlon paused.

"Hey, I know I don't know much about hiking and camping," he said, "but our science teacher was just telling us that certain types of water can have bacteria in it. Is this water safe to drink?"

Nadia paused and placed her canteen at her side. "You know, you're right. I completely forgot about that." She rummaged through her backpack. "I always carry a water filter in case of emergency. It filters out bacteria and other stuff when we drink from it."

After a moment, Nadia pulled out what looked like a huge handheld straw. She frowned.

"Oh geez, it's busted," she said. "It must have broken when we took the tumble down the hill."

Marlon took off his backpack. "Let me check mine," he said. Moments later he pulled a massive straw out of his own pack. "This is what we need, right?"

Nadia grinned. "Yep! You're a lifesaver, Marlon!"

"Thanks! Feels good to actually help for a change," Marlon replied.

He handed Nadia the purifying straw first. She knelt down and dipped the straw in the water, taking a few big gulps.

"Oh, that's good," said Nadia. She handed the purifying straw to Marlon, and he took a few big sips as well.

Once they'd finished drinking, Marlon stuck the purifier back in his bag. They might need it again.

After that, he and Nadia finished putting on their backpacks. Then Nadia pulled a map of the trail from her pocket. She unfolded it so they could look at it together.

"What are these little triangles with numbers all over the map?" Marlon asked, studying the paper.

"They're markers that are placed around the woods and trails. If people get lost, they can look at a map, get their bearings, and figure out what they're close to," Nadia explained.

Marlon turned around and looked in the distance. "There's a sign a little ways down the river," he exclaimed. "I'll be right back!"

He set off, and sure enough, about forty steps away, there was a marker attached to a pole in the ground.

Marker fifty-seven, Marlon said to himself. He quickly turned around and made his way back to Nadia. "We're near marker fifty-seven!" he announced.

Nadia looked over the map. "I found it!" she said. "We can hike three miles south, along the hillside. That should lead us back to the regular trail and put us a few miles away from our cabin!"

"That's great!" Marlon said. He exhaled a sigh of relief.

But his relief didn't last long. Colt began to growl. The dog was focused on something.

"Hey, what's wrong, Colt?" Marlon asked.

He and Nadia looked up from their map, and at the same time, they both froze. There, blocking their path back to the cabin, was a baby black bear. It was eating Marlon's trail mix.

Nadia looked alarmed. "I thought you put your snacks in the bear bag!" she said quietly.

"I meant to!" Marlon whispered back. "But then we started talking about water straws and how to get out of here, and I got distracted."

The bear was just a cub, but even Marlon knew what that meant. Where there was a cub, there was likely a mother bear close by.

Black bear mothers were very protective of their young. If she arrived and thought Marlon or Nadia was a threat, things could get ugly quickly.

Nadia took a deep breath, but her hands were shaking. "We have to stay calm," she said. "Do not panic."

Marlon didn't even have time to panic before things went from bad to worse. A larger bear—probably the cub's mother—lumbered out of the trees.

Colt let out a whimper. Marlon wanted to whimper too. They were in serious danger.

CHAPTER 8

BEWARE OF BEARS

"What do we do?" Marlon asked.

Nadia kept her voice low. "I did some reading about bears in the area before we came on the trip," she said. "We have to stay calm. Start slowly walking backward, away from the bears. Keep eye contact with them to see how they react. Do not run. Keep walking back until we're out of sight."

Leaning down, Nadia scooped Colt into her arms. That way he couldn't run off.

"OK," Marlon replied. "But they're blocking our way back. How are we going to get back now?"

"Let's figure that out once we're away from the bears," Nadia said. They began to slowly walk backward. "It's important to talk to them in a calm voice so the mom doesn't view us as a threat."

Marlon nodded. He was willing to do whatever Nadia said if it meant getting out of harm's way.

"Hi, bears," Nadia said. "Please have the trail mix. We hope you like it. We mean you no harm. Easy there. Easy now."

The mother bear stayed close to her cub. It was still happily rummaging through the bag of trail mix. Marlon, Nadia, and Colt crept backward, staying close to the river, getting farther and farther away from the bears.

After a few minutes, they were around the bend, out of the bears' sight.

"Do you think we're OK now?" asked Marlon.

"I don't know," said Nadia. "The mama bear can probably still smell us. And bears have a great sense of hearing. But if she wanted to chase us, she probably would've done it by now."

"You learned all this stuff about bears from the trail website?" Marlon asked. He was impressed.

"That, and I had to write a report on them for school a while ago," Nadia replied.

Marlon was tempted to stop and check the map to figure out where they were going. But even though he could no longer see the bears, he heard a low, deep growl through the trees.

"What was that growl for?" asked Marlon.

"I don't know, but the farther away we are from it, the better!" Nadia said.

Marlon nodded. The map would have to wait.

CHAPTER 9

HELP!

Marlon and Nadia kept moving until they'd put some safe distance between themselves and the bears. Only then did they stop to check the map.

"Let's keep heading north," Nadia said, studying the route. "There's a trail shelter that way."

Marlon nodded in agreement, and the kids and dog set off. Eventually they made their way back to the main trail. It had taken much longer than expected, but they'd avoided any more wild animal encounters.

"I can't wait until we get to the shelter," Nadia said as they walked side by side. "I love the outdoors, but this is too much for even me. What's the first thing you're going to do after we get back to our parents?"

"Take a long shower," Marlon said with a laugh. "Then eat some pancakes. Trail mix is fine and all, but I need some actual food."

"Same here," Nadia said as Colt began to bark. "I think Colt wants some real food too."

Marlon and Nadia laughed as they continued toward the shelter.

"Thanks again for helping me survive this," said Marlon. "I would have been lost out here without you."

"You helped too," Nadia said. "I wouldn't have wanted to spend the night out here alone either."

"You wouldn't have had to if it wasn't for me," Marlon reminded her.

Nadia smiled. "That might be true. But think how much you learned," she told him. "You managed to set up and break down a tent. And you had a working water filter."

"I guess you're right," Marlon said. "Parts of it were even kind of fun."

"It's OK to have fun in the great outdoors," Nadia agreed. "You just need to be aware and prepared too."

After a few miles, they passed marker fifty-four. "Almost there!" said Nadia, taking the lead.

"That's great, I can't wait to—" Marlon's voice suddenly cut off. He and Colt both yelped as they fell.

"Marlon?" Nadia said, turning around.

Where Marlon and Colt had been moments before was a hole about three feet wide. It was hidden from sight by the taller grass along the trail.

"Down here! We're down here!" Marlon yelled. Colt barked and yelped.

Nadia stared down into the hole. From up above, it seemed extremely deep. She could just barely make out Marlon and the dog at the bottom of it.

"Are you OK?" Nadia called.

"I don't know," Marlon called up to her. "My ankle hurts a little. I broke Colt's fall, so he's OK."

"Can you climb out?" asked Nadia.

Marlon stood up slowly. His ankle was throbbing, and the hole was damp and muddy. He tried to get a grip on the thin roots along the wall, but it was too slippery. Every step he took sent him sliding back to the bottom.

"I can't climb up. It's too slick," he called up. "Do you have any rope in your backpack?"

"Hold on!" Nadia said.

She took off her backpack and pulled some rope from one of the compartments. She tossed one end down the hole, but it was too short.

"This isn't going to work," Nadia said, frustrated. "Listen, the shelter isn't that far away. I'm going to get you some help. Hold on. I promise I'll be back!"

"Be careful!" Marlon yelled.

Nadia took off running in the direction of the shelter. As she ran along the grassy trail, she kept an eye out for any other holes. She didn't want to end up like Marlon.

Suddenly, over the hill she spotted a small wooden cabin with windows and an overhanging roof. The shelter!

Nadia ran even faster to get to it. Within moments, she was at the front door and quickly opened it.

A ranger looked up from her desk as Nadia burst in. "Are you OK?" the ranger asked. "What's wrong?"

Nadia panted for breath. "My friend and I got lost yesterday," she said. "We were on our way here when he and our dog fell into a big hole! I think he hurt his ankle really badly!"

The ranger shook her head. "Those old trap holes are everywhere. Hunters used to use them to trap animals. Every time we think we've filled them all, another one pops up. Don't worry, we'll get your friend and your dog out of there."

The ranger gathered her crew. They grabbed a rope ladder and a first-aid kit.

"Show us where your friend is," the ranger said.

"Follow me!" said Nadia.

* * *

Marlon and Colt sat in the hole, waiting. "I hope Nadia's OK," Marlon said, looking at Colt. "What if she got trapped too? Then who's going to rescue us?"

Colt began to lick Marlon's face. "OK, OK, I'll stop worrying," he said.

Suddenly Marlon heard a rustle of footsteps and people talking. Then he heard Nadia's voice. "Hold on, Marlon!" she called.

A moment later, a rope ladder fell in front of Marlon and Colt.

"Are you OK?" another voice called. Marlon looked up to see a ranger peering down into the hole from above.

"I think so. But I can't put a lot of pressure of my left ankle," said Marlon.

"That's OK, we'll come down and get you out of there," the ranger replied.

"I told you I'd be back!" Nadia shouted. "I got us plenty of help!"

The rangers used spikes to secure the rope ladder. Then the lead ranger went down to rescue Marlon and Colt.

"Thank you so much for helping us," said Marlon when he and Colt were back on the trail.

"That's what we're here for," the ranger replied. "Now tell me, how did you kids end up out here all alone?"

Marlon and Nadia exchanged a look. "It's a long story," they said in unison.

CHAPTER 10

SAFE AND SOUND

Inside the ranger's office, Marlon's and Nadia's parents waited for their children. As the door opened, they jumped up. Nadia and Colt walked in with Marlon limping behind them.

"Nadia, you're OK! Thank goodness!" Nadia's mother exclaimed. Her parents swept her up in a big hug. "We're so glad you're OK. We had search parties looking all over for you two!"

"Have a doctor look at Marlon's ankle," the ranger said. "He may have a bad sprain."

Marlon's parents held tightly to their son.

"Mom, Mom, I can't breathe. You're hugging me too tight," Marlon said.

Marlon's mom eased up a bit. His dad gave him a big hug. "You had us worried, son. What happened?" he asked. "And where did you find this dog?"

"This is Colt," said Marlon. "We found him the first night that we were lost and—"

Before Marlon could finish, Colt bolted out of the office.

"Hey!" Marlon yelled. "Where are you going?"

He limped back out of the office. Nadia and their parents followed. Outside, a little girl and her family surrounded Colt.

"Colt! There you are! I've been worried sick!" The little girl held Colt close, then turned to Marlon and Nadia. "Are you the ones who found my dog?"

"Yep," said Marlon.

"Colt is really smart," said Nadia. "He alerted us about bears!"

"Bears?" Marlon's mother repeated.

"I'll explain it all later," Marlon said, "but first I owe you and Dad an apology. It was my attitude and behavior that got Nadia and me into this mess. The wilderness is no joke, and the trail can be dangerous if you're not paying attention."

"I wish it hadn't taken getting lost on the trail to teach you that lesson, but I'm glad you understand now," Dad said. "But more than anything, I'm just thankful you're OK."

"Marlon helped us find a way back," Nadia chimed in. "Plus he learned how to set up and break down a tent. And he saved us from dehydration with his water filter!"

Marlon blushed. "I guess I did learn some things, huh?" he said.

"Can we get something to eat?" said Nadia. "We're starving! All we've had to eat is trail mix."

"And after that, if my ankle is OK, can we walk the actual trail tomorrow?" said Marlon. "I really want to learn more about it. Even though we've had a rough time, I think I'm starting to like the outdoors."

Marlon's parents looked shocked. "Really?" Mom said.

Marlon nodded. "But for now, can Nadia and I have some pancakes?"

AUTHOR BIO

Shawn Pryor is the creator and co-writer of the all-ages graphic novel mystery series Cash & Carrie, writer of *Kentucky Kaiju*, and writer and co-creator of the 2019 GLYPH-nominated football/drama series Force. He is also the author of the Jake Maddox Sports Stories title *Diamond Double Play*. In his free time, Shawn enjoys reading, cooking, listening to music, and talking about why Zack from the *Mighty Morphin Power Rangers* is the greatest superhero of all time.

ILLUSTRATOR BIO

Alan Brown is an English illustrator working in children's books and comics. His love of art started as a young boy, when he had unlimited access to comics at his gran's sweetie shop. These days, he can be found busy at his desk, illustrating with help from his two sons and dog.

GLOSSARY

bacteria (bak-TEER-ee-uh)—very small living things that exist all around you and inside you; some bacteria cause disease

canteen (kan-TEEN)—a small metal container for holding water

dehydration (dee-hy-DRAY-shuhn)—a life-threatening medical condition caused by a lack of water

enthusiast (in-THOO-zee-ast)—a person who is very excited about or interested in something

filter (FIL-tur)—a device that cleans liquids or gases as they pass through it

incline (IN-kline)—a slanting surface

lush (LUHSH)—covered with a thick growth of healthy plants

ranger (RAYN-jur)—a person in charge of a park or forest

shelter (SHEL-tur)—a safe, covered place

steep (STEEP)—having a very sharp slope, almost straight up and down

torrential (taw-REN-shuhl)—coming in a large, fast stream

unison (YOO-nuh-suhn)—at the exact same time

DISCUSSION QUESTIONS

1. Imagine you and your family are going hiking on the Appalachian Trail. What is one thing you would most want to see or do while hiking? Talk about what it is and why it's important to you.

2. Marlon and Nadia were lucky to escape from the danger of the black bear and her cub while making their way back to camp. What other types of scary situations do you think could happen while hiking? Talk about some possible dangers.

3. In this story, Marlon struggles to put up the tent until Nadia gives him a hand. Think about something you struggled to accomplish until you received help from someone else. Talk about what it was, who helped you, and how that made a difference.

WRITING PROMPTS

1. Have you ever taken a hiking trip or camped out? Describe your experience in a few paragraphs. If you haven't done either of those things, then describe what you would like to do during your hiking or camping trip.

2. It can be interesting to think about a story from a different point of view. Try writing Chapter 5 from Colt the dog's point of view. What was Colt thinking about when he jumped inside Marlon and Nadia's tent?

3. Marlon's parents wanted him to spend less time on his phone and more time enjoying the great outdoors. How do you think Marlon felt about that at the start of the story compared to the end? Write a few paragraphs explaining how his attitude shifted after his hiking experience.

THAT'S A LOT OF HIKING

The Appalachian Trail is more than two thousand miles long and runs across the eastern United States. It is the longest hiking path in the world. It travels through fourteen states: Georgia, North Carolina, Tennessee, Virginia, West Virginia, Maryland, Pennsylvania, New Jersey, New York, Connecticut, Massachusetts, Vermont, New Hampshire, and Maine.

Nearly fifteen thousand people have hiked the entire Appalachian Trail, which can take five to seven months to complete. The elevation changes along the trail make completing the hike the same as climbing Mount Everest sixteen times over! (The summit of Mount Everest sits at 29,029 feet.)

According to the Appalachian Mountain Club, the Appalachian Trail crosses a road every four miles. Along those roads are many small mountain communities, which can make it easier to find your way back to civilization. In some areas, the Appalachian Trail runs straight through many towns or passes within a few miles of other towns.

WHAT ABOUT THE BEARS?

Black bears live and pass through almost all parts of the Appalachian Trail. Bears usually avoid people, so an encounter is unlikely. But if you're in black bear country, it's better to travel in a group. (You don't want to move through a bear's habitat silently or alone.)

If you do happen to come across a black bear, know what to do. Here are a few tips:

- Keep a safe distance. Give the bear as much space as possible. If you can, go back the way you came. If you have to continue, give the bear a lot of space.

- Identify yourself by speaking calmly and firmly so the bear knows you are a human, not prey.

- Stay calm. Stand your ground but slowly wave your arms in the air. This will make you appear larger and more intimidating.

- Walk, don't run, and keep your eyes on the bear so you can see how it's reacting.